STERLING and the distinctive Sterling logo are registered trademarks of Sterling Publishing Co., Inc.

Library of Congress Cataloging-in-Publication Data
Kirwan, Wednesday.
Minerva the monster / by Wednesday Kirwan.
p. cm.
Summary: Feeling out of sorts, Minerva pretends to be a monster,
but after realizing that monsters do not eat cookies, read stories,
or sleep in nice warm beds, she decides to rejoin her family.
ISBN-13: 978-1-4027-5718-1
[1. Family life—Fiction. 2. Boston terrier—Fiction. 3. Dogs—Fiction.] I. Title.

PZ7.K6397Mi 2008
[E]—dc22
2007043376

2 4 6 8 10 9 7 5 3 1

Published by Sterling Publishing Co., Inc.
387 Park Avenue South, New York, NY 10016
www.sterlingpublishing.com/kids
Text and illustrations copyright © 2008 by Wednesday Kirwan
The artwork was prepared using gouache and colored pencils.
Designed by Lauren Rille

Distributed in Canada by Sterling Publishing
c/o Canadian Manda Group, 165 Dufferin Street, Toronto, Ontario, Canada M6K 3H6
Distributed in the United Kingdom by GMC Distribution Services,
Castle Place, 166 High Street, Lewes, East Sussex, England BN7 1XU
Distributed in Australia by Capricorn Link (Australia) Pty. Ltd. P.O. Box 704, Windsor, NSW 2756, Australia

Sterling ISBN-13: 978-1-4027-5718-1

For information about custom editions, special sales, premium and corporate purchases,
please contact Sterling Special Sales Department at 800-805-5489 or specialsales@sterlingpublishing.com.

FOR MY MOM,

from her little monster.

"**I'M** a monster!" Minerva roared.

"Goodness!" said Mom.

"We've never had a *monster* in the house before!"

"Can you make me a monster costume?" asked Minerva.

"Let's see what we can do," said Mom.

Minerva drew huge monster teeth
and taped on pointy monster horns.
Then she colored the whole mask purple
with just the right number of green spots.

"**GRRRRRAAAAAARRR!!!**" rumbled Minerva.
She tramped out the front door
to find some monster things to do.

She pounced at the birds in the garden.

And stomped on the dry leaves in the yard.

And hung upside down by her knees from the ginkgo tree.

"Little Monster, would you put these letters in the mailbox for me?"

"Monsters don't mail letters!
Monsters growl at babies."
Minerva snarled at Keely.

Dad was raking leaves.

"If you're a monster, what happened to Minerva?" he asked.

"I ate her. She was delicious!"

"I see," said Dad.

Minerva crashed backward into the pile of leaves.

Minerva stomped back inside.
"Little Monster," said Mom,
"please pick up your crayons."

"Monsters don't even *use* crayons!" bellowed Minerva,
settling into the closet to work on her growl.

At dinner, Mom said, "Please eat your beans, Little Monster—they're good for you." Minerva's brother, Francis, had almost finished his.

Minerva grunted. "Monsters don't eat green beans.
They eat slugs, doodlebugs, and dragonflies," she said.
Mom sighed. "I'm starting to miss Minerva."

After dinner, Francis, Baby Keely, Dad,
and Mom played Crazy Eights together.
Minerva sat under the table.

"How's the cave?" called Dad.

"Okay," said Minerva.
"There are plenty of slugs down here."
But she was starting to feel lonely.

"Too bad monsters don't play games,"
Mom said. "Minerva usually wins."
"Too bad monsters don't eat cookies,"
Dad said. "The peanut butter kind
was Minerva's favorite."

"Too bad," Minerva whispered.

"It's time to put on our pajamas, kiddos,"
Dad said, laying down his cards.

"Monsters don't wear pajamas," growled Minerva.

"You're right," said Dad. "They have thick monster fur to keep them warm." He zipped up Keely's snuggly bunny pajamas and gave her a squeeze.

"That's right," said Minerva, but she was feeling a little cold and her corduroys were starting to itch.

"Time to hop into bed, sleepyheads," said Mom.

"Monsters don't go to bed . . ."
said Minerva, but she was
a little less sure of herself.

Minerva rubbed her eyes sleepily.
Francis looked very cozy in his soft, warm bed.

"Who's ready for a story?" asked Dad.

"Do monsters listen to stories?" asked Minerva.

"I don't know," Dad said. "I think monsters
live by themselves in dark caves,
without anyone to read to them."

Minerva imagined a cold monster cave deep in the woods.

She pictured all the lonely monsters
sleeping on rocks and stumps,
with no parents to tuck them in...

and not a single bedtime story.

"I'm not a monster! I'm ME!" shouted Minerva, ripping off her mask.

"It's good to have you back," said Mom.

"We missed you." Then she read Minerva's favorite story.

"See you in the morning, Minerva," said Mom.

"I'm not Minerva,"
said Minerva quietly to herself.
"I'm a tiger."